THE TREE
THAT CAME
TO STAY

Anna Quindlen
THE TREE THAT CAME TO STAY

illustrated by
Nancy Carpenter

Crown Publishers, Inc · New York

$\mathcal{T}$he day the tree came to stay,
the snow fell down with a hissing sound.

The children saw each flake, just for a moment, sticking to the car windows, and then the snowflakes melted and were gone. When the car climbed the big hill to the farm where they always found their Christmas tree, the wind whistled around them and they felt warm behind the glass.

"I want a Christmas tree that's as tall as the stars," said Bud, who was the biggest one.

"I want a Christmas tree that's as fat as Santa Claus," said Woo, who was middle-sized.

"Douy douy douy," said Bubba the baby, who was too young to know what she wanted yet.

When they got to the field, Dad took the saw out of the back of the car, the snow making white shadows on his shoulders. Mom tied Bubba's hat under her chin. Bud thought the trees looked like soldiers standing straight in their rows—blue spruces and Douglas firs and Scotch pines that had grown from little trees to big ones, just waiting for December.

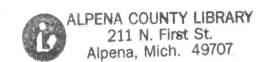

Bud walked slowly, looking closely at each tree, and he thought he saw one he remembered from the year before. It was taller now, just like him. Woo ran up and down, catching flakes in his cold fingers. "Baaa baaa baaa," said Bubba. Her red boot got caught in a little drift, and it came off, and she tumbled into a tree, her fat little arms around it to stop from falling, her white sock waving in the white air. Mom ran to rescue her.

"I think we've found it," said Dad, uncurling Bubba's little fingers from the tree trunk and lifting her high on his shoulders as he looked at the tree that had rescued her. And Bud circled around the tree that Bubba found, and he knew that Dad was right.

"It's not that tall, but I like it," said Bud.

"It's not that fat, but I like it," said Woo.

"Aaaah," said Bubba as Mom put her boot back on.

Bud thought it looked like a Bubba kind of tree. It was shortish and plump, a perfect triangle, and it made him feel good. The snow melted on its branches and dripped off like tears, and Bud could see silver in each drop.

"It looks like Christmas," said Dad.

So they took it home.

That night the children stayed up late so that they could decorate the tree. They put the silver bell, the tiny stuffed bear, the satin rocking horse, and the wooden soldier on its branches. They hung the red and silver glass balls and looked at their faces in them, their noses fat and their mouths wide.

Dad helped Bud lift the angel onto the top branch, and Bud felt as if he were flying. It was his favorite part of the decorating. When they plugged the lights in, the candle in the angel's hand lit up.

"Hooray," everyone yelled, even Bubba, and then they had
hot chocolate and went upstairs to bed.

"It's the best tree yet," said Woo as he looked back over his shoulder. And when they were in their beds and the lights were out, Bud could see it behind the black of his eyelids—the green branches and the white lights and the angel looking down on them all.

"It's the best tree yet," he said the next morning when they came downstairs in their pajamas with the rubber feet in them and saw all the boxes in their green and red and silver paper in piles beneath its plump green branches.

It was the best Christmas yet, too. Bubba got a bear made out of lamb's wool, and Woo got a dragon that breathed fire when it walked, and Bud got a model of a dinosaur with real bones. The Christmas before, Bubba hadn't even been born yet, and Woo was too little to really understand. Bud remembered the other Christmases, and the other Christmas trees, but when he thought about Christmas without Woo and Bubba, he knew he liked this Christmas best.

"I wish it could be forever," he said as they ate cookies shaped like Christmas trees with green sugar sprinkles on them.

"Nothing lasts forever," Mom said, but Bud wished Christmas could, and the tree, and the cookies, and he and Bubba and Woo eating them together.

But the Christmas tree lasted only a week, and then one morning, when the cookie tin was empty, Dad said it was time to take the tree down.

They took off the silver bell, the bear, the rocking horse, and the wooden soldier and wrapped them in tissue paper. They took off the glass balls and packed them away carefully in their boxes.

Dad held Bud high in the air, and Bud put his hands around
the angel's little waist and lifted her gently from the top branch.
The tree looked sad, with nothing on it but some bits of wrinkled
tinsel. Its branches were prickly instead of soft, and its green was
a little gray.

Dad carried it outside to the telephone pole beside the trash
can and laid it in the snow. The children came and stood beside
it. Bud hated taking the angel down, but he hated taking the tree
outside even more.

"Christmas is over," said Woo sadly.

"I hate it when Christmas is over," said Bud, his eyes scratchy.
He closed his eyes and tried to make the picture of the tree with
its lights and balls behind his lids again, but it only made him feel
sadder.

"Ohhh," said Bubba in a deep voice, and Bud thought it
sounded as if she were sad too.

Mom saw them from the window, and she came and stood with them and looked down at the tree.

"Nothing lasts forever," Bud said.

"Well…" said Mom, putting her arm around his shoulder, and she didn't say more for a long time. "Well, nothing stays exactly the same." Then she went back into the house, and when she came out, she had a basket in her hand. She knelt down next to the tree and ran her hand down each of its branches and a shower of pine needles fell into the basket. Soon the basket was full of needles.

"Smell," she said.

Bud put his face into the basket, and a sharp fresh green smell went into his nose. It was the smell of the tree farm, and of their living room on Christmas morning. It was the smell of Christmas!

"Christmas in a basket!" shouted Bud.

"Baaa baaa!" yelled Bubba, falling over beside the tree and putting a pine needle into her mouth.

Mom put the basket on the table near the back door, and on its handle she tied red and green ribbons left over from the presents. And at least once a day, when the children passed through the room, they stopped to smell the Christmas smell, and though it got fainter and fainter, there was always at least a little bit of it there. Bud even put a few needles in the bottom of his coat pocket, and sometimes, for no reason at all, he would bring them out between his fingers and sniff. And then he would smile. If Bubba and Woo were with him, he would let them smell Christmas too.

"Mmmmm," Bubba would always say, and Bud was sure she understood.

For Quin, Christopher, and Maria
—A. Q.

To Caryl, for making all of my
Christmases memorable
—N. C.

Text copyright © 1989, 1992 by Anna Quindlen
Illustrations copyright © 1992 by Nancy Carpenter

Published by Crown Publishers, Inc., a Random House company,
225 Park Avenue South, New York, New York 10003
Text originally appeared in a different form in the New York Times Magazine
in 1989.
CROWN is a trademark of Crown Publishers, Inc.
Manufactured in the United States of America

Library of Congress Cataloging-in-Publication Data
Quindlen, Anna.
The tree that came to stay / by Anna Quindlen : illustrated by
Nancy Carpenter.
p. cm.
Summary: A family finds a way to preserve the feeling of Christmas into the
new year by filling a basket with the pine needles from the Christmas tree.
[1. Christmas trees—Fiction. 2. Christmas—Fiction. 3. Family life—Fiction.]
I. Carpenter, Nancy, ill. II. Title.
PZ7.Q4192Tr 1992
[E]—dc20   91-31957
ISBN 0-517-58145-0 (trade)
0-517-58146-9 (lib. bdg.)
10 9 8 7 6 5 4 3 2 1   First Edition